Sam Goes to School

Written by **Mary Labatt**

Illustrated by **Marisol Sarrazin**

SCHOLASTIC INC.

New York Toronto London Auckland Sydney
Mexico City New Delhi Hong Kong Buenos Aires

Sam was bored.

She looked out the window.

Kids were coming

down the street.

A big yellow bus came.

"Kids are going

on that bus!" thought Sam.

"I want to go, too!"

Sam ran to the door

and pushed.

It was open!

"Here I go!" she thought.

Sam ran to the bus.

Kids got on the bus.

Sam got on, too.

Sam hid under a seat.

A girl looked down.

"A puppy!" she said.

"Don't tell!" said a boy.

"We can take this puppy to school!"

The girl put Sam in her backpack.

"Hide in here, puppy," she said.

"This is good," thought Sam.

"I am going to school."

The girl closed the backpack.

"Shhh," she said.

The bus stopped

and the kids got out.

The kids went into the school.

Bump, bump, bump went Sam

inside the backpack.

The girl opened the backpack.

"Stay here, puppy," she said.

"Here is a cookie."

"Yum," thought Sam.

"School is fun!"

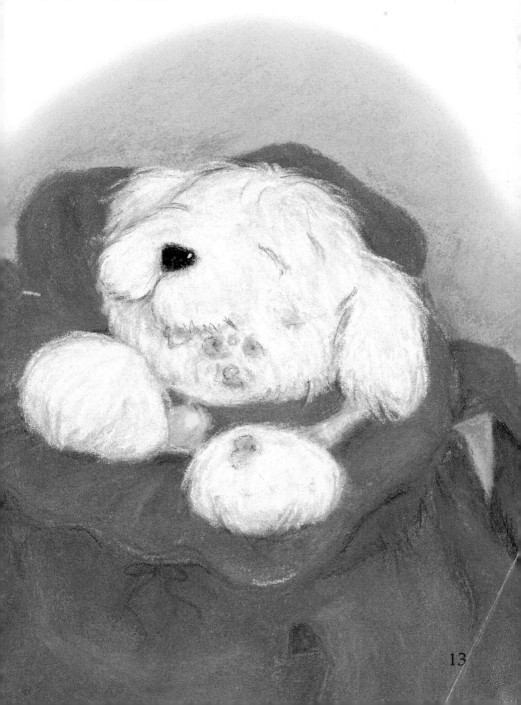

All morning the girl and boy

came to see Sam.

They gave Sam a sandwich,

some chips and a little cake.

But Sam got tired of the backpack.

"It is too dark in here," she thought.

"I am getting out."

Sam climbed out of the backpack

and peeked around the corner.

Sam saw lots of kids.

Kids were painting.

Kids were writing.

Kids were reading books.

The girl saw Sam.

"Oh, no!" she said.

"Oh, no!" said the boy.

But it was too late.

"I can paint with the kids," thought Sam.

She stepped in the paint

and walked all over the paintings.

"Oh, no!" said the kids.

"I can write with the kids," thought Sam.

She grabbed a paper.

Then she ripped it up.

"Oh, no!" said the kids.

"I can read with the kids," thought Sam.

She pulled a book off the shelf.

Then she chewed on it.

"Oh, no!" said the kids.

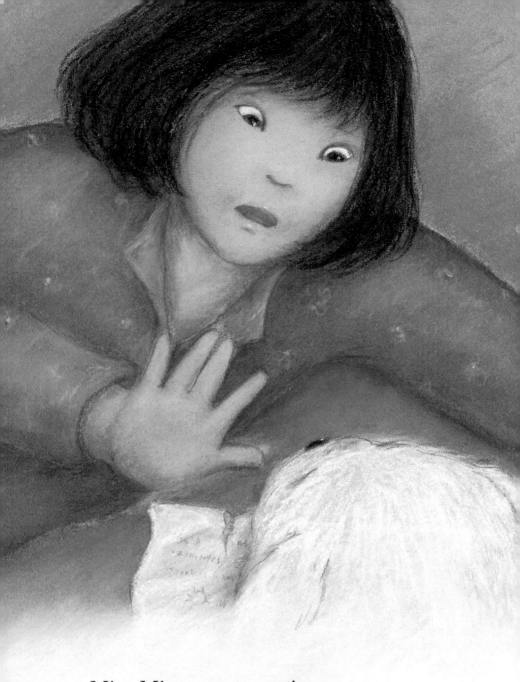

Miss Min came running.

"No, no, no!" she cried.

Miss Min picked Sam up

and looked at her tag.

"This is Sam," she said.

"Here is her phone number."

"I have to call Sam's family," said Miss Min.

"And we have to clean up Sam's mess."

Miss Min put Sam in a box.

"Sam can watch us

until her family comes," she said.

"No more painting for Sam."

Sam watched the kids.

Kids were writing.

Kids were painting.

Kids were reading books.

And kids were petting her!

Then Joan and Bob ran in.

"Sam!" cried Joan.

"How did you get here?"

"She came on the bus," said the girl.

"Woof!" said Sam.

"On the bus!" said Bob.

"The bus is not for puppies!"

"No," said Miss Min.

"Dogs cannot come to school."

"No dogs in school!" thought Sam.

"That is not fair!

School has kids.

School has painting.

School has cookies.

School has chips and cake!"

"Puppies need school, too!"

ISBN 0-439-67954-0

Text copyright © 2004 by Mary Labatt. Illustrations copyright © 2004 by Marisol Sarrazin.
All rights reserved. Published by Scholastic Inc., 557 Broadway, New York, NY 10012,
by arrangement with Kids Can Press Ltd. SCHOLASTIC and associated logos are
trademarks and/or registered trademarks of Scholastic Inc.

12 11 10 9 8 7 6 5 4 3 2 1   4 5 6 7 8 9/0

Printed in the U.S.A.   23

First Scholastic printing, September 2004

Edited by David MacDonald
Designed by Marie Bartholomew